Clarion Books · New York

For all Kitties
everywhere

Calligraphy on jacket and title page by Paul Shaw.
Clarion Books
a Houghton Mifflin Company imprint
215 Park Avenue South, New York, NY 10003
Text copyright © 1993 by Wendy Watson
All rights reserved.
For information about permission to reproduce selections from
this book, write to Permissions, Houghton Mifflin Company,
215 Park Avenue South, New York, NY 10003.
Printed in the U.S.A.

Library of Congress Cataloging-in-Publication Data
Watson, Wendy.
Happy Easter day! / by Wendy Watson.
p.   cm.
Summary: A story in which a family prepares for and enjoys Easter,
combined with both traditional and literary rhymes.
ISBN 0-395-53628-6
1. Easter — Literary collections.   [1. Easter — Literary collections.]
I. Title.
PZ5.W29Hap   1993
808.81′933 — dc20
92-27921   CIP   AC

HOR   10   9   8   7   6   5   4   3   2   1

Hippity, hoppity, Easter's almost here!

Hot cross buns, hot cross buns;
One-a-penny poker,
Two-a-penny tongs,
Three-a-penny fire shovel,
Hot cross buns.

We bake hot cross buns with Mom.
Mmmm!
Doggie likes hot cross buns, too—even the raisins.
Doggie, do you know that Easter is coming?

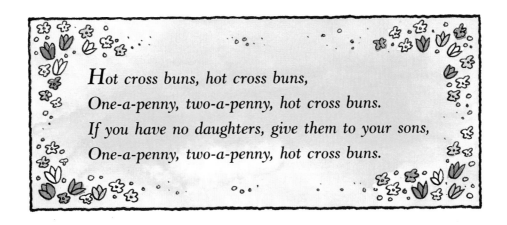

Hot cross buns, hot cross buns,
One-a-penny, two-a-penny, hot cross buns.
If you have no daughters, give them to your sons,
One-a-penny, two-a-penny, hot cross buns.

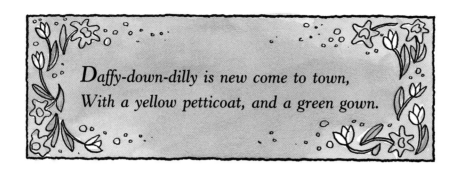

Daffy-down-dilly is new come to town,
With a yellow petticoat, and a green gown.

We go shopping for our Easter clothes.
Everyone gets something new.
Kitty, get off!
You can't sleep here.
We're saving these for Easter.

At Easter let your clothes be new,
Or else be sure you will it rue!

Cuckoo, cuckoo, cherry tree,
Catch a bird and give it me;
Let the tree be high or low,
Let it hail or rain or snow.

Dad helps us make an egg tree.

It has tiny buds.

Inside the buds are new leaves.

We plant grass seed around the bottom.

Is it Easter yet?

No, but it's getting closer!

March winds and April showers
Bring forth May flowers.

We go to Grandma's barn for extra eggs.
Everything is hatching and growing at once.
We see baby chicks and baby rabbits,
baby lambs and baby plants.
Does that mean Easter is here?
Not yet.

Chook, chook, chook, chook, chook,
Good morning, Mrs. Hen.
How many chicks have you got?
Madam, I've got ten.
Four of them are yellow,
And four of them are brown,
And two of them are speckled red,
The nicest in the town.

Little Blue Ben,
Who lives in the glen,
Keeps a blue cat,
And one blue hen,
Which lays of blue eggs
A score and ten;
Where shall I find
The little Blue Ben?

We decorate eggs,
even Grandpa, Grandma, and kitty.
Look at all the colors!
We hang some eggs on the egg tree.
Easter *must* be almost here.

At last, it's Easter eve!
We fill our baskets with grass.

We put the colored eggs in a big bowl.
Everything is ready.

Is that the Easter bunny?
Shhh!
Quick, go to sleep.

It's Easter morning!
Look—bunny tracks.
And chocolates!
And there's a jelly bean.

Ooops! Doggie got it first.

Now let's see how many eggs we can find.

We'll leave some for kitty.

And our Easter baskets must be here *somewhere*.

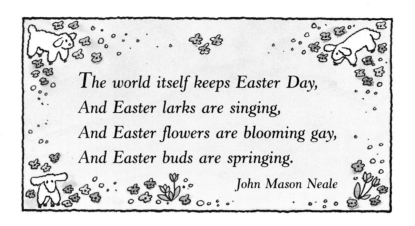

The world itself keeps Easter Day,
And Easter larks are singing,
And Easter flowers are blooming gay,
And Easter buds are springing.

John Mason Neale

After breakfast, we put on our Easter clothes.
Don't we look beautiful?
We walk to church.
The whole world is dressed for Easter.

Snowdrop, lift your timid head,
All the earth is waking.
Field and forest, brown and dead,
Into life is breaking.

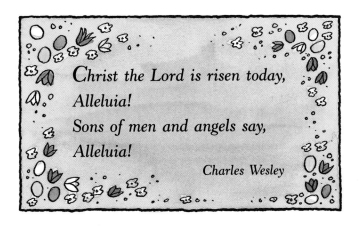

Christ the Lord is risen today,
Alleluia!
Sons of men and angels say,
Alleluia!

Charles Wesley

The church is filled with flowers.
The organ plays exciting music.
We sing as loud as we can.
Everyone is glad that Easter is here.

Here is the church,
Here is the steeple,
Open the door,
And see all the people.

Grandma and Grandpa come home with us
after church.
They bring new flowers to plant in our yard.
We all sit down for dinner.
Everything tastes good,
but we like the lamb cake best of all.

For the beauty of the earth,
For the beauty of the skies,
For the love which from our birth
Over and around us lies,
Lord of all, to thee we raise
This our hymn of grateful praise.

Folliott Sandford Pierpoint

Round about there
Sat a little hare;
The bow-wows came and chased him
Right up there!

After dinner,
it's warm enough to play Easter games outdoors.
That's lucky, because we drop a lot of eggs.
Doggie, aren't you getting full?

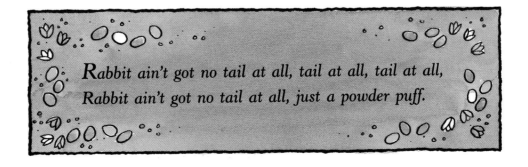

Rabbit ain't got no tail at all, tail at all, tail at all,
Rabbit ain't got no tail at all, just a powder puff.

Now Easter Day is over—
almost.

"Mew, mew, mew."
What's that?

Kitty!
This is the best Easter surprise of all.
Happy Easter Day!